THE WONDERFUL JOURNEY

THE WONDERFUL JOURNEY

For Gontdawgie,
the Woman who flew away

THE WONDERFUL JOURNEY
A RED FOX BOOK 0 09 948307 6

First published in Great Britain by Hutchinson Children's Books
an imprint of Random House Children's Books

Hutchinson edition published 1999
Red Fox edition published 2000

1 3 5 7 9 10 8 6 4 2

Copyright © Paul Geraghty, 1999

Red Fox Books are published by Random House Children's Books,
61–63 Uxbridge Road, London W5 5SA,
a division of The Random House Group Ltd,
in Australia by Random House Australia (Pty) Ltd,
20 Alfred Street, Milsons Point, Sydney, NSW 2061, Australia,
in New Zealand by Random House New Zealand Ltd,
18 Poland Road, Glenfield, Auckland 10, New Zealand,
and in South Africa by Random House (Pty) Ltd,
Endulini, 5A Jubilee Road, Parktown 2193, South Africa

THE RANDOM HOUSE GROUP Limited Reg. No. 954009

www.**kids**at**randomhouse**.co.uk
www.paulgeraghty.net

A CIP catalogue record for this book is available from the British Library.

Printed in Hong Kong

THE WONDERFUL JOURNEY

Paul Geraghty

RED FOX

My grandma came to live with us from a long way away. Every Wednesday she took me to the railway yard to see the trains. If it rained, we sat in an empty shack beside the railway. And there, to the smell of steel and the shudder of the engines, she would tell me stories from the far away places she used to live.

One day she told me a true story.

'Do you remember,' she said, 'the time I told you that I would fly away?'

I remembered. She had been telling me about the place where she was born. She seemed to be looking a long way past the sun. 'One day,' she had sighed, 'I will fly back home to where I came from. And then I will be happy.'

I knew she could fly.

'Aren't you happy here?' I asked her.

'Not really,' she'd said, but she never told me why.

'Well,' said Gran, 'that time has come.
Time for me to fly away.'
'But you can't go,' I cried.
'Time doesn't stand still,'
she said. 'I can't
stay forever.'

'Then can I come with you, Gran?'

'No, Sam,' she said kindly, 'you belong here with Mum and Dad. And you still have many stories ahead of you.'

'But Gran, who will tell *your* stories?'

'Why, you will,' she said. 'Look at that old engine. How many times have we imagined where it would take us?'

'Besides, you can still see me if I go away,' she went on. 'You can see me from the other side of the world, whenever you want!'

I laughed at her. 'People can't see *that* far.'

'Oh, but they can,' said Gran. 'Didn't you know?'

When she told me that, I felt a tingle run down my neck, right to my toes.

'Would you like to see Africa right now?' she whispered.

We closed our eyes and she told me a story: we were flamingos, flying high across the sky.

Over the sea we flew, above green mountains and a hot, baking desert, till we were too tired and thirsty to go on. So we rested with the other birds in our favourite steamy lake.

'Not long now,' said Gran, 'till our migration is over.'

And off we went again, this time high over villages, rivers and forests until vast open plains appeared below.

We landed near a pride of lions, resting beneath knotty trees and a great volcanic mountain.

'We are now very close to where I used to live,' Gran whispered. 'The sun met me every morning and the sound of the animals sent me to sleep at night.'

I wanted to go there. I wanted to look back and see if I could see Gran from the mountain.

Then Gran took us back to when she was a little girl.

'This is why I love coming here, to be near the trains,' she said. 'It reminds me of the journeys I took long ago to places that only the big steam trains could go.'

It was then that I knew I had travelled
with her many times before. Every story she
had told had taken me on a journey. We had
travelled together all over the world.

'So you see,' said Gran, 'you can travel any time you want, anywhere you wish.' She looked up at the sky. It was getting late. 'And right now I think we'd better travel home!'

I felt scared. I didn't want to go, in case I never saw her again.

'Don't be silly!' she laughed. 'Just remember, you can see me whenever you like.'

Then she gave me a big hug. 'This is our special goodbye,' she said.

That night I travelled on my own to strange,
and wonderful places that I had never seen
before. I knew then that I would always
be able to reach Gran, wherever she went.
And that she would always be able to
reach me.

Next Wednesday, Gran didn't come to fetch me. Instead, Mum gave me a letter. It said, 'Goodbye, Sam. Remember to think of me and remember our special stories. Lots of love, Gran.'

There were things I still wanted to tell her. So I hurried to the railway yard to see if I could catch her.

I looked in the shack where we had sheltered. I couldn't find Gran, but everywhere I looked were the stories we had shared.

Gran had flown away. But in the thunder of the trains, I could still hear her voice.